SIDNEY

Goes to School

Sharon Rentta

ALISON
GREEN
BOOKS

This is Sidney,

and these are his friends:

Gloria,

Rufus,

Oscar,

Neville

and Betty.

They play together . . .

. . . and they go to school together.

Their teacher is called
Mrs Dogsbody.

One day, Mrs Dogsbody said,
"We have a new friend joining
us today. This is Alfie."

"Hello, Alfie,"
said everyone.

Alfie seemed quite lively.
He was very keen to meet them all.

Next it was time for Show and Tell.
Sidney wanted to tell everyone that
he could ride a bicycle.

I've got a
thing to tell!

But Mrs Dogsbody said,
"Let's hear from Alfie first."

Alfie said, "I can do this . . .

and this . . .

and this . . .

and this . . .

and this!"

Everyone said,
"Oooh!" and **"Aah!"**
Everyone except Sidney.

Aah!

Ooh!

Ooh!

When Mrs Dogsbody said, "Did you want to tell us something, Sidney?" Sidney said, "No, thank you."

Suddenly, riding a bicycle didn't
seem that exciting any more.

Everyone **loved** Alfie.

So Sidney did a naughty thing.

Eek!

Then he did **another** naughty thing.

And then, at playtime,

he did a **really** naughty thing.

Sploosh!

Ow! I'm all wet!

"Sidney!" said Mrs Dogsbody. "If you can't play nicely with the others, then you'd better play on your own for a bit."

So Sidney did.

Sidney sat under his box
for a long time.

When a voice said, "Hello!"
Sidney said, "Go away!"

"Why don't you like me?"
asked Alfie.

"Because you're good at
everything and I'm not good
at anything," said Sidney.

"That's not true," said Alfie. "You're good at being a friend. All the others really like you."

"Really?" said Sidney.

"They want you to come and play," said Alfie.
"Gosh," said Sidney. "Do they?"
Together, he and Alfie ran over to join them.

"Your trunk is really amazing," said Alfie.
"Thank you," said Sidney.

Good header!

Come and play, Sidney!

Go, Sidney!

Go, Alfie!

Everyone was playing football.
"I'm on Alfie's team," said Sidney.
"We're friends now!"

Good kick, Sidney!

To me!

For Joshua and Hannah –
two little monkeys!

First published in 2010 by Alison Green Books
An imprint of Scholastic Children's Books
Euston House, 24 Eversholt Street
London NW1 1DB
A division of Scholastic Ltd
www.scholastic.co.uk
London ~ New York ~Toronto ~ Sydney ~ Auckland
Mexico City ~ New Delhi ~ Hong Kong

HB ISBN: 978 1 407108 56 8
PB ISBN: 978 1 407108 57 5
Printed in Singapore

1 3 5 7 9 8 6 4 2

Papers used by Scholastic Children's Books are made from wood
grown in sustainable forests.